Maqbool

Other works of **AKHILESH** published by Rajkamal Prakashan :

Maqbool (Maqbool Fida Husain Ki Jeevani)

Achchambhe Ka Rona (Kala-Lekh)

Aap-Beeti (Mark Shagaal Aatmkatha)

Daraspothi (Kala-Lekh)

Akhilesh : Ek Samvad (Piyush Daiya)

Sheershak Nahi (Kala-Lekh)

Maqbook Fida Husain (Kala-Lekh)

Dekhna (Sansmaran Evam Anya Kala-Lekh)

Maqbool

Akhilesh

Translated from the Hindi by Rahul Soni

BANYAN TREE BOOKS PVT. LTD.

Price : ₹450

First edition : 2017

Published by:
Banyan Tree Books Pvt. Ltd.
7/31, Ansari Road, Daryaganj
New Delhi-110 002 (India)
www.rajkamalprakashan.com

Printed at :
B.K. Offset
Naveen Shahdara, Delhi-110 032

ISBN : 978-81-905401-3-1

for

Saiyed Haider Raza

Content

Look, There's Husain

1.

I am the sound of silent feet, listen closely and you will hear…

Meeting Maqbool Fida Husain is like meeting a century. I've met him many times and have many memories of those meetings, I also recall his way of working and so on. He is almost always immersed in his work. In fact I don't think I've ever met him while he wasn't painting, or that he ever lets a morning or an afternoon or an evening go past without creating. It's impossible to imagine him not painting. While he was filming *Gaja Gamini* he would make time to paint even in the middle of a shoot in a special studio he had erected on set. In my experience all painters have their own way of working – but Husain is unique. He has dedicated himself fully to painting. He is a true, mature and complete painter.

I began to relate to him as a painter in 1974, when he came to Indore. I was studying at college. When my friends and I heard he was in Indore we hurriedly made plans to organise an exhibition and invited him to inaugurate it. His attractive personality and mesmerising presence made it a memorable event for us. For Husain being a human and being an artist go together – you cannot separate them. And he is both an extraordinary human and an extraordinary artist. You always see these two sides of him together. For instance he could say, 'Let's go have tea,' immediately after inaugurating an exhibition and head out in search of some small tea shop in Bombay Bazar that he remembered from when he used to live here, and there we'd drink tea and return to the exhibition venue. That's the kind of personality he has, in which nothing is important but everything has importance. Polite, courteous and so full of life. Pulsating every moment, in every moment creating the unexpected and unimaginable.

Another time he came to college and said he wanted to make a painting and gift it to the institution. We arranged for a canvas and he began to paint. He began from the lower half of the canvas. There was an erotic charge to the shapes he made, it seemed like he would make an erotic painting. But as the painting began to fill out it turned out to be the deity Ganesh. There was nothing erotic about it but his approach to art made it seem so. Only Husain could think of painting like that, to start from anywhere and take it anywhere. He has the ability to take any line, any shape, any colour and turn it into something else. I have many such stories from my meetings with him, each time I see him in a new way. From him I have learnt that there can be no readymade model for creativity. Even at the age of ninety-five he creates with a speed and an energy impossible for any other painter to match. Impossible at least for me. This magical ability resides only in him and only for him. His memory, his sense of humour, his intellectual rigour remain strong and unshakeable. He is always willing to share and discuss ideas, but his own positions remain firm.

2.

When I was young there were two things that struck me about Husain. First, that he was a famous painter. Second, that he always walked barefoot. It seemed like a contradiction to me and aroused a curiosity about him in my heart. Later when I grew to know him as Husain, he came to my house and the first thing I did was look at his feet to see if he was wearing shoes. His feet were bare. My friends and I wandered about Indore with him for three days and while we kept our shoes and slippers on he seemed quite comfortable without. Soon after that something else happened. He was awarded the Padma Shri and went to receive the honour from the President of India barefoot. The press tried to sensationalise the matter stating that it was against the code of conduct, that it was an insult to the President and so on. I came to know later that he had given up wearing shoes in 1964 at the funeral procession for the poet

Muktibodh. Muktibodh was his friend and he gave up this one thing in memory of his friend without a second thought. He told me about a prank he'd played once: 'One day I wore a white shoe in one foot and a black shoe in the other and went to visit all my painter friends. Not one of them noticed! I had to point it out to them as I left – look, I'm wearing mismatched shoes!' That was his mischievous nature at work. And the irony was that these were all his painter friends for whom *seeing* was crucial but none of them saw. And some of them are very famous painters indeed.

He is a great storyteller. And this too becomes a sort of story he told: the day he went to visit his friends wearing one black shoe and one white shoe. If he hadn't become a painter he would certainly have become a great writer. Telling stories always gives him pleasure and he weaves and embellishes them in his own unique way. He has written many postcards to his friends telling them stories using both words and pictures.

3.

When we were at college we all wanted to be like Husain one day. He was our inspiration and our ideal. That was also the time when we began to study his work carefully. His art emerged from a background of Indian culture. At that time we weren't able to grasp the depth of his work but his attractive personality held sway over us. We would look at his paintings, not understand, and look again and keep on looking. That was part of our study. I had some of his books at home, early books that were filled with sketches, collages, paintings, etc. I never tried to copy them though. His paintings, his lines, what we were taught about them – I was influenced by it all of course but I never felt the need to imitate. Whereas a lot of my friends and older painters would make copy after copy of his work. Husain's horses were famous in the art world. And in Indore there were many painters who only made horses, either exact copies or just a little different. But these were not horses they had seen themselves and so they remained lifeless. When Husain painted them, the special way in which he captured their energy and speed was beautiful. And this was because they had emerged from his cultural context. Husain's horses were born from the Duldul horse that led Muharram processions in Indore. For him the horse was a symbol of deep belief and also of a culture. Other values associated with horses like power, etc. were also attached to it of course. His horse was the Duldul horse, but it was also the Uchchaihshravas that emerged from the churning of the ocean. On the other hand what the other painters made were merely copies of Husain's horses which is why they all lacked power, lacked life. There is an anecdote from those days that I like a lot. Someone asked him, 'What are you doing nowadays?' He said, '*Main ghode bech kar so raha hoon*' – an expression in Hindi that means 'I'm sleeping soundly,' but literally translates to 'I'm sleeping after having sold my horses.'

Those days we used to find Husain's physical presence more attractive than his creative presence. Our attention was drawn to his creative presence for the first time when a book published by the Tata Institute arrived at our college. Perhaps he sent it himself. Our principal Chandresh Saxena called us to his office to show us. It was a thick book. We flipped through it and pictures and photographs flitted past one after another until we came to a painting with the title *Between Spider and Lamp*. Saxena sir told us that it is an important painting and that we must study it carefully. So we gazed at it for a while. But it was of no use. We didn't know what we were looking at. We didn't even know that this was a painting that had changed the course of contemporary art in India. We wanted to turn the page and move ahead. Saxena sir said, 'Look carefully, there are curse words written on the painting.' And there were indeed some signs and letters towards the top. We wondered why a well-known painter would do such a thing. And in our eagerness to seek out these curses, we actually began to *look* at the painting. It turned into a ritual: we'd come to college in the morning and go straight to Saxena sir's office and begin hunting for the curse words. And in so doing I began to form a relationship with the painting, I began to see the things that made Husain Husain. His pictorial language became clear to me. I was never able to find the curse words but the painting got etched into my memory. I asked Husain about it in a conversation years later. He said, 'At that time I had three lovers. Those three letters are the first letters of their names.' But in that painting they did not remain mere letters, they turned into signs and as Swami used to say, in a painting a sign doesn't stay a sign but turns into a symbol, so they turned into symbols. Anyway that's when I began forming a relationship with Husain's art and it has only deepened over the years because of Husain's continued presence and the things my father told me. I began to see how his figures are related to Indian sculpture, to statues from the Gupta period and to the metal sculpture from the Chola period, to contemporary Indian folk culture, and to the very beginnings of art. To modernity and Indian tradition.

We became close because of two reasons: one, he was a good friend of my father's and two, because whenever we met our conversation always revolved around the world of contemporary art. I wasn't interested in anything else and so we only talked about things that were to my mind essential to art. I never talked to him about unimportant things or debates and topics of the moment. All my time with him was spent in serious creative conversation.

4.

A painter is surrounded by forms, natural and mechanical, but his memory on which he relies holds the experience, the distillate of forms, in essence and in physical relationships.

Whenever I meet Husain he never forgets to ask me how my work is going, what I am up to, whether I have any exhibitions on. He worries about what I'm doing. His other worry used to be my job at Bharat Bhawan. He had said from the start, 'Leave it, it's not good for you.' Whenever we met he would ask me, 'When are you quitting that job?' On one occasion he came home and made a sketch of a falcon, inscribing it with a line from Iqbal's poem: 'You're a falcon, your work is flight.' That's what he told me to do – fly. When I finally left my job he was the happiest person. This sort of concern for me on his part also deepened our relationship. It is his generosity that he cares so much and worries so much for an insignificant painter like me. There are other painters too but he doesn't have a relationship like this with anyone else. Those relationships end with one meeting. I find moral support in him. And he has always indulged me as well. For instance the exhibition titled *Anaadi* that I had organised in Delhi with Ratnottama Sengupta. We were displaying the works of forty-five painters from Madhya Pradesh. Why not have Husain sahib inaugurate it I thought. So I went to meet him and he said, 'Yes, why not? I'll do it.' I said, 'And since you are inaugurating it, would you please sign the invite too?' He said, 'Yes, why not?' I had prepared a draft of the invite which said, 'Eminent artist M.F. Husain will inaugurate the exhibition.' When he saw this line he said, 'I'm not eminent. I'm not even an artist. How can I sign this?' I said, 'But you are an eminent artist for us and this invitation goes out from us. These are our words not yours.' And he said, 'No, but the signature is mine. It's not right.' He was very reluctant and it took me a long time to convince him but he finally signed the invite though he still did not agree. On the day of the exhibition I called him and found out that he was still in Mumbai. I reminded him that he had to inaugurate an exhibition that evening. He said, 'I forgot. I'm in Mumbai.' And then at two o'clock he suddenly arrived and stayed on until five, talking to the artists, looking at the paintings, giving advice on how best to display them. Everyone was overjoyed that he was there, drinking tea with them and talking about their work. The exhibition was inaugurated informally in this manner and at five o'clock he went back to Mumbai. The formal inauguration was done by the guests who came in the evening. But he had kept his word. There are many things about Husain that make him unique, things that you won't find in any other painter. Extreme affection and instantaneous withdrawal are Husain's peculiar characteristics. Complete interest and complete detachment are his qualities. Among all painters, Husain stands apart because of these qualities – and perhaps that's what makes him Husain. I say 'perhaps' only because there must be other qualities I haven't been introduced to yet.

5.

I remember a man coming home at six in the morning bearing jalebis in a basket when I was a child. He possessed an extremely attractive personality, a glowing presence and a magical energy. We all ate the jalebis. Many years later when I knew him as Husain he came once more at six or seven in the morning, again bearing jalebis. That was when I made the connection with that childhood memory and realised this was the same person. He always came to visit early in the morning at six or seven, and always with hot jalebis.

He inaugurated a group show for me and my friends in the early seventies. One of my friends owned a sweet shop and it's interior was being redone at that time. There were two art galleries in the city but when we went to inquire we found out that they were both booked. We sat in the shop – the one which was being redone – and despairingly pondered over what to do. Then the man who was doing the interior spoke up: 'Why don't you have the show here? I'll turn it into a gallery.' And he did so overnight. We couldn't recognise the place the next day. We held our group show there and Husain inaugurated it. He loved its unusual location.

We were this little group in Indore and whenever some painter visited the city we would organise a show and invite him. In this way we'd get a chance to spend a few private hours with those painters. Only one painter refused us and that was N.S. Bendre. He didn't come to inaugurate the group show nor did he come to look. We told him it would run for three days and to please come visit any time but he didn't. Interestingly this was the same Bendre sahib whom Husain thought of as his guru. Husain never forgot that it was Bendre who first recognised his gift and went and talked to his father, insisting that Husain apply to art school. He never forgot this debt.

6.

As I begin to paint, hold the sky in your hands, as the stretch of my canvas is unknown to me.

Husain came to all of my exhibitions except for one group show that we did in Mumbai in the nineties: me, Harshvardhan Swaminathan, Bhagwan Chauhan and Sudhakar Yadav. I had called him up as usual and said, 'Baba, we're displaying our paintings, please do come.' He asked me where it was and I said, 'Jehangir Art Gallery.' 'Where's this Jehangir Art Gallery?' he asked and I immediately understood that something must have happened between Baba and the gallery. Later I found out that the Jehangir Art Gallery's committee of so-called artists and connoisseurs had blacklisted him. The reason was his exhibition *Shwetambari* in which he stretched out a white cloth across the gallery and scattered thousands of torn newspapers on the floor. It was perhaps his first installation. The amount of discussion it generated is a separate matter but the art gallery's committee did not like the fact that Husain held an exhibition there without displaying any paintings. And so they blacklisted him. It took them three years to reverse this decision and Husain was given gallery space once more. He brought in three trucks full of trash to display. I don't think he ever exhibited in Jehangir Art Gallery after that. Anyway. I called him three or four times to come to our show but he didn't come. On the day it ended he called me to say that he would be coming tomorrow and when I told him that the show had ended, that today was the last day, he said, 'In that case why don't you all come to my home. Tomorrow morning for breakfast, all four of you.' So we went in the morning and chatted away until one o'clock, forgetting all about breakfast. When we left Harshvardhan Swaminathan said, 'I'm starving.'

7.

Husain and I have many conversations about Hindi literature. He has a deep interest in poetry and is friendly with many poets. His world brims with literature. We often talk about poetry. Even on the phone, apart from other things, we discuss who is writing good poetry nowadays or the books and poems we have recently read. It's a creative hunger that he shares with his friends. He is in constant conversation with his own self. Husain's prose is a painter's prose. Years ago he wrote a poem for Swami's journal *Contra.* The language of the poem is a painter's language. Only a painter can write a line like 'whose brown burns in me.' Published in 1966 the poem *Cracks in Rembrandt* goes like this:

I am aware of
Cracks in Rembrandt
Whose brown burns in me
Though
Rock-rust boots
Are ditched-deep
Yet
The silky sun there
Shrills me

Husain's experience shines through in his prose. He doesn't try to make intellectual arguments or establish theoretical positions. In my opinion he doesn't think there's any position that needs to be established. Indeed, he has often expressed the desire to burn his paintings before he dies. That's how he sees the creative world, as temporary and meaningless, as nothing more than a momentary spark in eternity. That's the attitude he has towards his prose as well and he uses it in the same way: something suddenly occurs to him and he writes it down. Recently in London he told me about a new chapter he'd written for his autobiography. It was called *Two Rotis*. It's not an exposition on or a description of the amount of hard labour he had to do in his life to earn two square meals a day. It's about the importance of two rotis in the life of man, any man. And the sum of his experience in all its honesty speaks through his prose. His sense of humour too can be seen here. He doesn't write about life's big mysteries but about little everyday things that he experiences in all their reality and truth. The bitter and sweet moments of the life that he has lived, the life that surrounds him, they all become a part of his writing.

Another special characteristic of Husain's writing is his capacity to poke fun at himself. He doesn't take himself seriously. When you meet him you don't feel like you're meeting a great painter, one of the most important painters of the century. You can relax in his presence, be yourself. That's the kind of atmosphere he creates. Where conversations can happen. You can see this in his prose too. He is neither self-conscious nor careless about this. When he writes it is in full awareness of what can be gleaned from it. His writing is not dry, it's full of flavour much like his paintings. Whether it's his autobiography or some lines he's written about an exhibition or a series that he has thought about or some idea that has come to him while painting – his writing is pure, interesting and gripping. Yet its spontaneity is always evident. For instance he'd written a poem about *Gaja Gamini*. The poem is about his mother but he talks about Madhuri Dixit. In the end, because in his heart the image of his mother is incomplete, 'Madhuri' becomes 'Ma Adhoori' (or 'Incomplete Mother') – he expresses this beautifully. This connection between Madhuri and his mother formed in his heart. He was six months old when his mother died, and when he met Madhuri she was the same age as his mother. He has no memory of what his mother looked like nor did he ever paint her. There is never a face in the many images of mothers that he has painted. There is no reflection of it in his memory. So he does not paint it. The other women he paints all have faces. This is an unconscious attachment. Take his paintings of Mother Teresa. He has met her, has walked around with her, gone to the streets in Calcutta where she served. But he never drew her face. The bands of blue colour that form Mother Teresa are depictions of his mother. He has drawn many people, and he had met Mother Teresa and could easily have drawn her in the same way. But because he sees his own mother as a universal mother figure, he doesn't draw her face. This is an unconscious decision, something rooted very deeply in him. In her absence, his mother is present. She's there but doesn't have an identity. This also comes through in his poetry.

His language is populated and influenced by all things, poetry too, and couplets from Urdu and Persian. He knows these languages well. Once the *Times of India* printed a painting of his on the front page for the new year. Later when I met him I mentioned this painting, wanting to see it. He said, 'You know what inspired it? A line from Shamsher Bahadur Singh's poem *Patjhar*: '*Ek peeli shaam / patjhar ka zara atka hua patta.*' Husain understands this metaphor, its knottiness. The language of his painting has deep connections to literature. During everyday conversations he will recite a couplet in Persian and explain its meaning. His language is well-crafted, polished and at the same time it possesses a sense of humour. He is capable of using all contemporary contexts and talking about any subject, whether it is some word that has fallen out of use or cinema or politics or sports. His graciousness is wondrous, his beauty deep. He never operates at a level that is trivial. From his sentence construction to his topics of conversation, and of course when it comes to his own art – he is incapable of making any trivial gesture. Husain's being is the being of the whole century. This deepens his experiences, gives meaning to his seeing, reading, understanding. And that's what makes it interesting and pure for the listener and viewer as well.

These poems by Husain stand as proof:

❑

I feel a cup
Close to be burning colours
in my fingers—
They are burnt and alive.
For years my restless fingers
Had scratched the earth-bones
Never a starved streak of light
could live
in the midnight womb—
jade midnight—chiselled.
I am no more deaf
to the silent murmurs
Of a shapely clay being baked.
On the edge of my cup
I feel you close

❑

The feet nailed on earth
Are never tired.
The follow
The roaming echo . . .
Echoes once treasured
Behind caves and carvings.

Blown up rocks
Have not returned.
Though
Flooded passenger trains
Keep on shuttling . . .
making deep grooves on earth.

Millions pour in

To the burning colours
In my fingers.

Grooves deepen
Trains snail down.
Layer under layers,
Till the pores are blockes.

But the roaming echo
Do knock
The closed window.

❑

Tou have spent
The mountains there.

White river valleys
Weep over the distant days.

Blind windows . . .
Stuck on faces . . .
Wide open
Stare at each other.

There in the midst
Of matchmakers

❑

Why days come to me
When my yellow eyes in grey head
Could never be closed
Under the bed-sheet of nights.

I wish . . .
the failings of five months.
Swallow up the unborn years.

Let the histories
cut across me . . .
Without me

The key has lost one tooth.

And unlocked frontiers . . .
Restless . . .
Have gone to embrace
Their beloved country.

❑

In the neighbourhood
Of your breath
I have travelled close and far.
The wall there,
Sun-baked and brown
Paints a thin shadow
Over your lips.
Under that shadow
I remember,
How met
Are our najed words.

8.

I can say without any hesitation that if there's someone after Mahatma Gandhi who has truly known India it is Maqbool Fida Husain. Gandhi recognised the power of

India's people, Husain recognised the power of India's culture. He absorbed the whole spectrum of Indian culture and gave it expression through his art. The Indianness of Husain's art is that of an Indian. He didn't have to try to attain it nor was it thrust upon him – it is the very life of his paintings where folk and myth are woven together. He does not search for Indianness, he creates it. No other painter has been able to forge this sort of deep connection with India. Most of them seem to spend their creative lives in some sort of dilemma. If there's anyone else who has engaged with these matters it is Swaminathan. But he forged a connection with his traditions, with the tradition of humanity, on a different level – which is the abstraction of these cultural layers. This deep connection can be seen in the work of both painters. In their own ways both of them create the living, breathing, inclusive culture of India in their paintings. This culture doesn't belong to any specific community or circumstance, this is the culture of the human species – a realisation that glimmers in their paintings.

By the time Mahatma Gandhi came back to India he was already famous because of his activities in Africa. He had written *Hind Swaraj*. On his return he met Gopal Krishna Gokhale whom he considered his guru. Gokhale told him that although he had come back to India he knew nothing about the country. He asked Gandhi to refrain from speaking about Indian politics until he had spent a year traveling through the country, getting to know the people whom he would be fighting for. Gandhi took his advice and traveled for a whole year and that was when he truly felt the power of India's people.

In 1947 when India became independent, a lot of young painters, Husain's contemporaries, went to different parts of the world – London, Paris, New York – in order to the see the art there and learn from it. They thought, now that we are an independent country, we need to figure out what the roadmap for contemporary art in an independent country should be. It was a question that vexed and occupied everyone. Their motives were as pure and nobel as Husain's. But contrary to everyone else Husain went into the villages of India. He followed Ramlilas to see and understand them, he met people, tried to understand folk culture in all its different forms, he drew them, he became a part of them, and by putting all of his energies, all of his self into this, he absorbed the plurality of India into his very being. This he did at a time when his contemporaries were looking to French or Mexican art in order to replace the influence of British art, instead of looking to their roots, their tradition, their culture for inspiration.

The work Husain had been doing alone and without fanfare since 1948 found forceful expression much later in 1963, in the manifesto of Group 1890. It stated that, 'To us creative expression is not the search for, but the unfolding of personality.' It gives primacy to individuality in *seeing*. For the first time in Indian art Indianness was seen as a mark of self-respect rather than a cause for embarrassment. Octavio Paz was so affected by these young painters that he wrote the catalogue for their exhibition.

In the world of Indian painting Husain seems to be the only artist who was able to find his self profoundly right in the middle of his own culture. And the result of that is there for all to see in the form of his art. We see its influence in the contemporary art world which Husain created on the strength of his belief. No one came forward to help him in this. If there is anyone who appears to stand with Husain in some way it is Swaminathan. Sharp in his intellect and ideas, he also says the same things but many years after Husain.

In 1955-56 Husain began the work that had been developing in his mind since 1948 when he saw an exhibition at the National Museum. There he witnessed the ultimate emotional expression of Indian sculpture in the Gupta era statues and the bronze figures of the Chola era. Husain's folk consciousness was disrupted by the strength of these classical forms. He combined the naturalness and unselfconsciousness of folk culture with these classical forms and inaugurated Indian modernism. Later Swaminathan would also follow this path, where the expression of humanity was the highest aim. This common ground between Husain and Swaminathan was established much later. What is worth noting is that Husain had already created a framework for modern painting to which Swaminathan would later provide an intellectual base. Swaminathan emphasises a human creativity that withstands the horrors of its time and looks upon the canvas as a rising sun. The strength of the human species is in its creative expression, in which individuality is expressed not social reality. Swaminathan's creator rebels against the 'obscene social realism of Raja Ravi Verma and the ideal rural pictures of the Bengal school'. At the same time Husain talks about holding the sky in his hands. His creator also gestures towards this infinity where the sun rises. And that's what Husain was creating in his paintings. Husain created this world of modern art alone, which benefited not only my generation but generations to follow.

The first image in the heart of any young painter entering art school is that of Husain. It's from him that they acquire the strength of will and attempt to move forward in this direction. The light Husain alone spreads still sets aflame the hearts of young painters arriving many years later.

Apart from Husain's relation to his culture and apart from his experience, the time he functioned in is also significant. He was able to create an independent pictorial language for an independent country, whose subjects are many – from religious beliefs to political upheavals, from daily routine to important events. It is difficult to think of any painter who did the kind of work for his country's art that Husain did. And that is his important gift to us: he created modern Indian art, but he also planted the flag of Indian cultural identity around the world. The national museum of any country will have Husain's work whether they have the work of any other Indian artist or not – and in great numbers too. Husain registered his presence in this manner as well. It is a way of life for him, being constantly active and creating and exhibiting art around the world.

9.

I think what Husain puts of himself into his paintings is a distillation of his experiences of the various cultures of the country. Andhra Pradesh's culture is special in a different way from Bengal's. Rajasthan's folk culture is different from Madhya Pradesh's tribal culture. This variety, or should I say plurality, of Indian culture can be seen in Husain's work. Whether it is *Shwetambari* or his collages or paintings, an Indian Husain is clearly visible in everything, in the way a Bengali, a Malayali or a Gujarati is Indian even though they are different from one another. Yet they are steeped in Indianness in their own special ways. This is the same kind of oneness that Husain's images convey. It is the inviolable core of his work, whether it is his brightly coloured collages or the earthy colours that he is known for or paintings where he uses the human form or all those paintings that we instantly recognise as Husain's or the films that he makes, be it *Minaxi* or *Gaja Gamini* or *Through the Eyes of a Painter*. In all of these, Husain's vision is an Indian vision. It is the vision of a person who holds in himself the vastness of his culture. Here variety is not a weakness but a strength. There is a oneness that springs from a plural cultural sensibility and Husain's art is dedicated to that. Whereas his contemporaries spent their lives focusing only on one part of the whole, Husain found it impossible. He puts himself on the line every time, where there's the ever present danger of being swept away or drowned. He never backs down from taking risks as an artist and as a creative being. This ability to put himself on the line with every work is what makes Husain special.

We also see him stumble in his earlier work. He is not afraid to fail and he doesn't hesitate to show even these unsuccessful paintings. From 1955-56 when he found a clear language for himself, all those images begin to appear in which he went on to give form to Indian society, to give it meaning. When India became independent in 1947 it had no visual language of its own. India's creative heart was floundering and almost extinguished. It had lost its beliefs, its artistic traditions. This broken, scattered, lost creative heart needed firm, undaunted and fearless support. There was a similar fragmentation and directionlessness in India's social life which found support in Gandhi. The way Gandhi was able to inject a self-confidence into the people of India, in the same way Husain nurtured and nourished India's cultural consciousness which the British had destroyed with cunning expertise. If Husain had wanted to he could have accepted the existing so-called Indian art but he did not and instead started searching for new ground. He thought deeply about the kind of creative world Indians were going to inhabit after independence and began to work towards creating it.

10.

With the cooperation of the British, Raja Ravi Verma managed to get calendar art on the walls of every home in India. They kept saying that this is Indian art and we also began to look for our identity in his art. Even today many people believe that calendar art is the original Indian art. But this is the British way of looking at our culture. Raja Ravi Verma was not talented. He was an ordinary painter who started the use of oil paints. To think that he is a great painter just because he had a printing press and managed to get his pictures into every home shows not only a lack of knowledge but is also a kind of slavery. His work is the work of a weak painter, his imagination fails him. His paintings are proof of his failures. He belonged to a royal family and had the patronage of the British, he had the resources to start a printing press, he could make many copies of his paintings easily available – and he did. Even Husain's early paintings do not belong to this category. They are different. They are paintings of human feeling. They are the paintings of a man who would go on to hold the sky in his hands, whose creations would spring from infinity.

There used to be small shop selling art supplies in Indore. In that shop there used to hang a small landscape painting made by Husain in 1933 or so. This was when Husain was about to leave Indore. The painting depicts a landscape in Malwa. The picture consists of three dark stains on dust coloured paper. It is a bird's eye view of the Malwa landscape. It is abstract. Only the three stains can be seen spreading out from a deep colour at the centre and becoming lighter at the edges. They could even be three trees. If you saw it, it conjured up the pure essence of the Malwa landscape in your mind. This was in 1933 when Raja Ravi Verma was very popular and had dozens of imitators. But Husain didn't imitate him, he just made three stains. This was risky work. Imagine a young painter in 1933 standing in opposition to the debris of realism all around him – he makes three stains on dust coloured paper and steps into an unknown world of art where many would later follow him. This was Husain's creative hunger. This landscape emerged from that same hunger. For years I kept looking at this image. In the eighties Husain asked the shop owner if he could take the picture back and give him another. He painted a horse on a big canvas and gave it to him and took this small painting in return and went away. Eventually it got lost. And the painting that he had given the shop owner got stolen.

The point is that at a time when Raja Ravi Verma ruled the Indian art scene there was one young painter who was determined to not walk down paths that already existed but create his own. Bendre was also active at the time and he deeply influenced Husain. Husain considered Bendre his guru but he was not a follower. What he was immersed in was a search, was the process of seeing things in his own way. It is important to note that Husain saw, knew and understood what was already there, and only then decided to reject it and develop his own language. He looked for it and he found it, and in the process he took Indian art to a place of freedom, balance and involvement which his contemporaries were also searching for but could not find. Husain often called Bendre his guru but he was indebted to Souza as well. Both of them had a great influence on Husain. But their influence can only be discerned in his conversations. Not a speck of it makes its way into his work. Bendre's sense of movement and Souza's abruptness are entirely absent from Husain's work. If there is a presence in Husain's paintings it is that of Dattatreya Damodar Devlalikar, Husain's teacher and the founder of the Indore school. Those who have seen Devlalikar's sketches know the character of his lines. They know the importance he gave them in his work. Husain must have seen them while he was still a student and they must have made a deep impression on his young heart. Later when Husain became Husain, his strong lines were seen as a defining characteristic. His lines are not the same as Devlalikar's — he has taken away their curves, their rhythms, their softness and harmony and instead has made them firm and hard and straight and strong. There's nothing similar about Devlalikar and Husain, his influence too is all but invisible. Husain searched for his own line and in 1956 he finally attained it.

11.

In later meetings while he was writing his autobiography, he would read to me — sometimes one chapter, sometimes another. One day he said, 'I've written it all now, and it will be published as a book.' I said, 'Then you must get it published in Hindi too.' He'd written his autobiography in Urdu and these readings had all happened during unplanned meetings. I said this and came away. A year later he called to say that the Hindi translation was ready and that I should come and edit it since he could see some errors in the text. And so I went. He gave the manuscript, translated by his friend Kamana Prasad, to me. I saw that the sentence constructions were not always correct and there were other problems. Some lines seemed to be missing too. I started editing and the process kept going on and on. I would stay for two or three days and then return. Then I'd continue when I went the next time. It got to be almost a year. One day I found that the manuscript I had been working on was lost. Husain said, 'I don't understand where it's gone. I can't find it anywhere.' He knew that I was coming and he must have started looking for it. And now it couldn't be found. He said, 'Come, let's go to Hyderabad. It must be there.' We searched in Hyderabad. It wasn't there. He thought it might be in Ahmedabad. He must have gone there at some point and searched. Once he called to say it might be in Delhi. But it wasn't there either.

During one of our meetings in Bombay he said to me, 'Why don't you write it? We've had so many conversations. Forget that manuscript — if it's lost it's lost.' One of Husain's many unique qualities was that he never looked back. I told him that I'd have to talk to him and record the conversations. He called Dadiba Pundol and said he needed to buy a tape recorder. Dadiba brought a pocket recorder over. Whenever I could get away from Bhopal I would visit him and we'd be together for two or three days. Then the next sitting would happen. This kept going on for some time. He became sick of the recording process. He said, 'Let this be. Just remember what we talk about — write down whatever you remember and leave the rest. I don't like speaking into a mic.' One day as we were talking, his son Owais came over with a manuscript. This was the same manuscript I had been editing in Hindi. Husain leapt up and said, 'Arey! We've been searching all over for this. When did you take it?' Owais was working on a film and perhaps he'd taken it for that. Husain immediately had multiple copies made. He gave one to Owais. I completed work on the manuscript and Rashida ji wrote in her hand, *Husain's Biography*. In the midst of all this our conversations had reached his wedding. I decided to end the book there. From his childhood to his marriage.

I never heard the recordings. All those tapes lie somewhere safe. I wrote this book from memory. Often I felt like I was paraphrasing. But when Bharat came to transcribe, the tapes couldn't be found. When the tapes were found, Bharat couldn't be found. The tapes are still lying somewhere…

12.

This book's structure was decided not before but after it was written. A progression can be seen therein. From Husain's childhood to his wedding. The reason for stopping at his wedding was that my meetings with Husain stopped after our conversations had reached that point. He left India to live abroad. Because of this the text only goes so far. And after consulting with him I decided that we'd end the book there as well. Earlier it had been decided that the book would be written after my conversations with him. These conversations took place between 1990 and 2001. There were long gaps between meetings and only a few of them were planned in advance. For the most part they were chance meetings that we would then extend by a few days. For instance if I happened to be in Bombay for a day and if I happened to meet Husain, then I'd stay on for a couple of days more and we'd find a few hours in which to record our conversation. The rest of the time Husain would be busy with so many things that he could entangle you in them. And if you got entangled it was quite possible that you'd find a whole month had gone past. He was a creative centre that could suck you in if you neared its orbit. His aura was powerful and irresistible. His levels of activity are unimaginable and impossible to understand unless you live with him and see it for yourself. Being active doesn't only mean painting, he could also be traveling from one place to another or sitting with you for hours at some restaurant or tea shop in a favourite corner of the city, talking. And whatever he is doing, you become involved in it, a part of it.

During this time the idea of the book also kept changing. We only decided on the structure of the book after I had written all the chapters and read them out to him. He hadn't recited the chapters of *Maqbool* fully formed. I too left out a lot of things. Like how he used to paint boxes in his childhood. In that era, painting boxes was a way of earning money in his community. He would make two or three paisa per box. He'd given me a long description of this but since I didn't see it fitting in the book I left it out. There were many other such incidents that Husain told me about but I chose not to include. Many things were added, many removed. Like the chapter *Mother*. That chapter did not emerge from any one conversation. In my conversations with him the mention of his mother could come up at any time. In his many memories of childhood in which his mother is absent, in which his new mother is present, in which both are absent or both are present. All of this I collected and organised in a chapter. I made no notes for this either. He kept telling me and I kept listening.

But more than his words I believe it was his imagination that became the basis for my writing. The images born from his words and the words born from those images, that's what makes this book different, makes it read like a story. The language for *Maqbool* came to me not simply as language, but as a picture language, and these pictures make or get transformed into signs. In trying to recreate the shape of Husain's life I have only taken the aid of imagination. The events that Husain told me about were all very scattered, often he'd add some part of an incident a couple of years later. It was only through this picture language that I could join those pieces and see them as a whole. Like pieces of a jigsaw puzzle, I joined them and made them complete. That is the reason for the story like quality of the language which took shape in my heart during my conversations with Husain. I was able to imagine the Indore of his childhood because I had roamed the very streets where he had grown up, I knew the schools where he had studied. Husain's house had also been very close to mine. All those places came to life before my eyes as Husain told me about them, when he said Sanyogitaganj I could see exactly where he would have gone. Of course things would be slightly different, some trees would have been cut down, some new constructions would have come up. When I look at my childhood I see so many open spaces there, spaces that could be filled with imagination, not the full, bristling concrete jungle of today. One day Husain asked me, 'You used to have a house here, where is it?' We had sold that house. The person who bought the house had it demolished. On one side of our house was a rest house, on the other side a school, and all around it was a road. It was like an island and a landmark for Husain en route to his house. Husain must have visited the area again at some point but because that house was no longer there he wasn't able to recognise anything. That day he told me, 'There were so many shops there, I felt as if I had come to the wrong place.' He was at the correct place of course but the scene had changed. So obviously he came back lost and confused. My childhood memories are full of those empty spaces spread out around my house and around Husain's house. And Husain's descriptions were very close to those images in my memory. The book's story like quality has emerged from these images. It's impossible now for a child to grow up in that environment and listen to Husain's story and write it down. Imagination will desert him. Everything has changed. Cement buildings, haphazard encroachment, unimaginative, impractical changes have become the hallmark of not only Indore but independent India's urban growth. No city now appears different in character to another. The Parsi neighbourhoods and streets that Husain used to walk through are no longer there. I myself can no longer recognise what this place has become…

The language of *Maqbool* takes its shape from the shape of Husain's life. This was possible only because I knew all the places that he talked about. When he talked about his grandfather's chimney workshop, I was there. I know the street where all these shops were. I used to go there and stand for hours, watching. Everything was like magic. Some very old person with expert hands would transform one thing into another. All this proved to be useful for *Maqbool*. This book has been written on the foundation of memory. These are all the chapters that were written, none were added, none removed. The current structure of the book was created with Husain. He wanted me to add my sketches to the text as well, abstract images that had no relation to the story. I wanted him to do the sketches himself. Once we even decided that he'd do the sketch that began each chapter and I would do the rest. Years later when we met in Dubai, he said he wanted to do new sketches for the book. That made me happy – I'd always wanted that. I went to London recently just for this but because he was always so busy the sketches weren't ready. This might be the first book about Husain in which he has done nothing, otherwise he has had a hand in the publication of every book about him. And now it seems certain that Maqbool will have no hand in *Maqbool*.

13.

According to Wagish Shukla, 'Writers are like prostitutes, their job is to attract readers.' So this is my first step as a prostitute.

I'm grateful for Husain sahib's affection and trust. Had he not ignored my innocence and ignorance and given me the opportunity to converse with him regularly, this book would not have been possible.

I am also grateful to all those friends who knowingly or unknowingly helped to improve this text.

My deepest gratitude to Krishna Baldev Vaid whose advice and suggestions for improvement have made it a purer and more interesting book.

Dr. Shivdutt Shukla who translated Husain's poem *Cracks in Rembrandt* for me in a very short time.

I am thankful to Shri Rahul Soni for translating 'Maqbool' in English.

My friends Udayan Vajpeyi, Madan Soni, Piyush Daiya, Om Sharma, Rakesh Shrimal, whose critical comments helped me keep this text on track.

Mother

He lay in his cradle looking at his mother or looking at the stars. The stars that shone in the sky looked just like the beads of sweat that shone on his mother's face.

His mother was always busy with household chores. But whenever he called she came to sate his hunger.

Her body, weak after childbirth, grew weaker still from all the chores. There was no older woman in the family to help her take care of herself.

His birth added to the number of men in the family. His mother was elated at the birth of her first child. Her sister had died during labour so she'd had numerous misgivings about her own pregnancy.

She didn't know that one had to take care of oneself even after giving birth. She only got a few moments of rest amidst all the household chores.

Her first child. Tiny. Skinny. With a broad forehead. With a face like hers. With eyes that shone. She loved his eyes. Those big, black eyes, how they stared. Like the eyes of Vitthal. His long, delicate fingers, so beautiful. She dreamed of him growing up to help her with her chores. A son dear to every heart. The light of all eyes. Embraced by everyone, loved by all. She would name him Maqbool.

Maqbool, dear to every heart.

Maqbool lay in his cradle and stared at his mother. At the stars at night. At the beads of sweat on his mother's face that shone like the stars.

He would wait eagerly for his mother. His mother would be surrounded by chores.

He wanted to walk by himself but all he could manage was to fling his limbs about. The cradle would rock as he made his attempts.

When he was six months old he stepped out of the cradle for the first time. His body trembled in anticipation of reaching his mother.

Maqbool did not know that the world in which he had taken his first innocent steps no longer contained his mother.

He got out of the cradle and looked for his mother all over the house. But there was only the hard sound of tin being beaten into shape.

His mother wasn't home. He went into the street. He wanted to catch the attention of every woman passing by. He cried. For a while there was even a lap like his mother's. Then the same cradle.

He came out of the street and searched through Pandharpur. There were lakhs of people, there was Vitthal all around. He cried and screamed but in the chants of 'Vitthal, Vitthal' his screams went no further than his own ears.

His eyes filled with tears and he could no longer see the stars. The shining beads of sweat had also disappeared.

Mother wasn't in the house. She wasn't in the street. She wasn't in the village. Who had come to feed him? Who was he searching for? Had he been dreaming earlier or was he dreaming now?

He isn't sure if he remembers this or if someone told him or if it was all just a dream.

Maqbool's father, Fida Husain, worked a smalltime job in Pandharpur. His grandfather Abdul sold lamps. There were four others in the house. His grandfather's brother and son. His father's brother, Murad. Large crowds would descend upon the small village on the day of the fair. Lakhs of people coming to Pandharpur to catch a glimpse of Vithoba, to be blessed. His grandfather Abdul would sell more lamps then.

His grandfather would prepare especially for the fair. He would start making chimneys and keeping them aside months in advance. On the days of the fair there would be large crowds and he'd sell many lamps.

It had been Fida Husain's second marriage. His first wife had died in labour. The second died six months after giving birth. They were sisters. After the death of his second wife Fida Husain no longer had the heart to stay in the village.

He decided to move to Indore. So they moved to Indore. Maqbool's first journey. In his grandfather's lap. Leaving the stars behind.

Maqbool would always wonder, did his grandfather tell him all this or did he hear it from his father?

His first journey. And he was completely unaware.

Grandfather

Boy. Maqbool.

Maqbool doesn't like being called *boy*. He doesn't remember when they left Pandharpur. His grandfather says he was six months old when he made that journey, his first, in his lap.

All through the journey he saw fallings stars.

Many years have passed since they came to Indore. He has since gone to many places holding his grandfather's finger. They live in the cantonment. Close to them is a neighbourhood called Ushaganj. A short distance from Ushaganj is the Parsi neighbourhood, next the Murai neighbourhood, then the butcher neighbourhood. Sanyogitaganj, the Parsi neighbourhood, Ushaganj, the Murai and butcher neighbourhoods – whether they make up the cantonment or whether the cantonment lies at their centre, he cannot tell.

There are no soldiers in the British cantonment.

He has seen all these neighbourhoods with his grandfather. He remembers the roads. The streets, the crossroads. The turns, the bridges, the gutters, the trails, the tamarind tree, the school grounds, he remembers them all. If he wants to he can go without his grandfather. But he hasn't tried to yet.

Wherever they were headed, his grandfather would always stop for a cup of tea at Acchan Mian's tea shop.

The red coals smouldering in the brazier would hold Maqbool rapt. He would stare at them without blinking. First they would appear red, then yellow, and as he watched they would turn white, absolutely white.

He loved watching this, the white emerging from the coal. After a cup of tea his grandfather would leave. But the white would stay on in Maqbool's eyes for some time. He would feel lost and, holding his grandfather's finger, would allow himself to be dragged along.

But his heart would remain with the coals in the brazier. Their changing colours. Magic. He realised that it wasn't just colours but even shapes changed while you stared at them.

While you stared, the stars turned hazy, then invisible.

Staring changed the scene.

It changed the colours.

It changed the shapes.

Maqbool began to look at the process of seeing.

This was magic that Maqbool could do.

All by himself and all the time.

There was magic in his grandfather's hands too. His skill in making chimneys was unbelievable. Beating the tin to straighten it, cutting and folding it to make a cylinder, attaching a base to it, setting a lid. Making a round duct for the wick, fitting that in, adding a screw to raise or lower the wick, making holders for the glass. He would watch the whole process, the order in which his grandfather performed them. Before his very eyes a simple piece of tin would turn into a shiny chimney. His grandfather seemed a magician. He made all of it look so easy.

Making chimneys was easier than making tea. He'd noticed this over and over again. Acchan Mian would sweat as he made tea, in fact he was soaked in sweat all the time.

The ease with which his grandfather made the chimneys was a sight to behold. As he worked, he talked, ate fragrant paan, met with friends and acquaintances who came to visit, and as he talked to them another chimney would be ready.

Like a magician reaching for a handkerchief in his pocket and pulling out a pigeon.

His grandfather is a magician.

If someone asks Maqbool about the things he wants to do, there are three things.

First, he wants to chew on fragrant paan like his grandfather.

Second, he wants to make chimneys.

Third, he wants to grow a white beard like his grandfather's.

The fragrance of the paan is intoxicating. Two kinds of fragrances emanate from his grandfather's achkan. First, the perfume of khas and second, the fragrant paan. The fragrance of the paan in his grandfather's pocket follows him. Or does he follow the fragrance? He doesn't quite know yet.

Whenever he has asked his grandfather's permission to chew paan he has been denied.

'You're too young.'

He hates that sentence. 'You're too young.' Everyone flings these words at him. And now when he wants to chew paan, his grandfather too. His father says it when he wants to accompany him to the mill. Whenever he wants to do anything people say, 'You're too young,' as if that's all they know how to say. Especially when they talk to him. They never use these words when they talk among themselves.

All those things he wants to do but his being too young makes impossible pass before his eyes.

Meaning:

He's too young to have fragrant kivaam.

Too young to make chimneys.

Too young to grow a beard.

Too young to climb the roof.

Too young to play on the road.

Too young to drink tea.

Too young to wander alone.

Too young to go to the mill.

Too young to wear an achkan.

He's too young. How young, he can never understand. Why isn't his grandfather too young he asks himself. His grandfather plays with him. What he does, his grandfather does too. Then why isn't he too young?

When father laughs grandfather says, 'You laugh like a child,' then why isn't his father too young?

It's a riddle without an answer.

But there's another twist.

He's also told, 'You're not a child anymore.' Just yesterday when there was too much chilli in his food and he didn't want to eat it everyone said, 'You should eat chilli. You're not a child anymore.'

This sentence too would be repeated many times every day. 'You're not a child anymore, go have a bath by yourself. Think for yourself. Pick it up yourself. Dress yourself. Tie your shoelaces yourself,' and so on. He'd hear these words on many occasions.

Maqbool's head would spin. He couldn't understand. Sometimes he was too old, sometimes too young.

Without having changed in any way he would keep turning from young to old and old to young. Want to make a chimney? Too young. Want a drink of water? Too old, go and get it yourself.

An annoyed young Maqbool and a confused old Maqbool would douse himself in cold water.

Young Maqbool, with old Maqbool hidden inside, would make lots of secret plans. That he'd make a chimney. When he grew up he'd make one for sure. Not just one, lots. Of all sorts.

That he'd grow a beard when he grew up. Just like his grandfather's. White like the stars. Soft like velvet. He thought his grandfather's beard was very beautiful. Shaped with great care. Glowing white like those embers of coal. Maqbool thought there wasn't a more beautiful and more alive human being in the whole world. No one wiser either. He had an answer to Maqbool's every question. The solution to his every problem.

An achkan, a white beard, a paan fragrant with kivaam, the perfume of khas.

His grandfather's personality was unique. When Maqbool went around holding his finger, he felt immensely proud.

He told his grandfather many times that he wanted to make chimneys, that he wanted to grow a beard, but every time he was too young.

'Have patience. Patience is god's greatest gift to us.' His grandfather presented this piece of advice on so many occasions it surprised Maqbool.

What was this troublesome thing called patience he could never understand. It annoyed him.

If you find some dish very tasty, have patience.

If you want to see something new that's come to the house, have patience.

If you're hungry, have patience.

Even to make a chimney, who knew how long he would have to be patient. If you want to play in the morning, have patience. Maqbool and patience were like the two ends of the earth — they could never meet.

He waited impatiently for the ability to be patient.

Chimney

One evening — young Maqbool stealthily, old Maqbool confidently, young Maqbool doubtfully, old Maqbool impatiently — entered his grandfather's workshop. His intentions were clear. He would make a chimney. Young Maqbool's heart beat wildly. A strange excitement made his limbs tremble. Old Maqbool, trying hard to control his every movement, muttering reassurances and encouragement, cast a sharp glance around the workshop.

Everything was familiar, everything recognisable. The place his grandfather sat at. The desk in front of him. The cupboard full of tools. The bench in the corner where he'd often sit and watch his grandfather at work. Everything was familiar, everything recognisable.

Old Maqbool confident like grandfather, young Maqbool hesitant, opened the tool cupboard. Before picking up the tools Maqbool rolled up his sleeves like his grandfather did. Young Maqbool was alert, his ears tuned to any approaching footsteps.

He took the tools out from the cupboard one by one and laid them out. Young Maqbool was in a hurry. If this task ended the others could begin.

He was alone here for the first time today. The workshop tools lay before him. Some chimneys hung ready, some lay half-done on the floor, and there was tin cut to size and kept aside for those yet to be made.

He is alone. There are the tools and there is the raw material. Spontaneously like grandfather, his hand reaches to stroke his beard. Young Maqbool finds that there is no beard there.

His fingers stay frozen mid-gesture for a moment.

He picks up the hammer. It isn't an everyday hammer, it looks different. It's so heavy he feels it slipping out of his hand. He is surprised.

He looks at it carefully. In grandfather's hands it waves in the air like a flower, going up and down so easily. How did it become so heavy? He is suspicious.

It has to be a different hammer. Otherwise why isn't he able to lift it?

Young Maqbool knows that it is the same hammer, it's just that he can't lift it. He looks in the cupboard for another and finds that it is the only one. Did grandfather work with such a heavy hammer? Maqbool suddenly feels pride at his grandfather's strength.

Old Maqbool started looking for the hidden hammer. Over and under and in front and behind the cupboard he searched but it was nowhere to be found. Giving up he turned to the shears.

The shears that looked tiny in grandfather's hands looked huge in his. He tried cutting through the tin. He pressed on it with all his might but wasn't able to even scratch the surface.

Nor was he able to mark the tin with the awl. It didn't curl on the stake. He wondered if grandfather had two sets of tools. For the past hour he hadn't been able to cut or curl the tin. The seamer didn't work either. He couldn't even lift the hammer.

He felt as if his hands had fallen on the wrong set of tools. Grandfather must surely have two sets, one to work with, one for show.

Maqbool was bathed in sweat. He looked all around. He knew the place was the same, the tools were the same. He despaired.

Acchan Mian could have made two cups of tea with the amount of sweat he'd produced. Was making tea easier than making chimneys he began to wonder.

Young Maqbool felt proud of his grandfather. He looked like an angel as he used these tools and created, as he watched, a magical chimney.

He would cut tin as if it were paper. It would curl into a cylinder. The hammer would wave in the air like a flower. The magical sparks would fly. It all looked like something from a dream, and when he opened his eyes his grandfather would have a new, shiny chimney made with his magic hands.

His heart began to beat normally as he thought of his grandfather.

He felt as if his grandfather's magic fingers had vanished his fear.

Maqbool looked at his own hands in despair. Small and soft with thin long fingers. His hands were smaller than his grandfather's.

Just today he had seen a newborn's hands. Compared to those incredibly small and beautiful hands he'd felt his were very big. He even thought they were big enough to make chimneys.

Which was why Maqbool had come here today. To make a chimney. But his resolve wavered. Maqbool repeated to himself: I will make a chimney today.

His tired gaze fell on his grandfather's pencil. For a moment he wondered if this too were a different pencil, if this too would refuse to work.

He used to sit next to his grandfather every day and draw something on paper with this pencil.

I will make a chimney today.

Maqbool repeated to himself.

He began to draw the chimney on paper. Who needs big hands to make a lamp he thought. His small hands moved swift upon the paper, and thoughts moved swift inside his mind.

A lamp in the imagination.

He was making a chimney.

He is making a chimney.

Maqbool is thinking.

He thinks.

Can we fill a paper lamp with kerosene?

He pours liquid from the pencil into the paper chimney.

Can you attach glass to a paper lamp?

He attaches transparent glass to the paper chimney.

Can you light a paper lamp with matchsticks?

He sets the paper chimney alight with the black of his pencil.

He could see his chimney burning. In the light of the chimney he could see his shape and the shape of the chimney. His hands trembled. He saw magic flow out of the pencil's sharp point. The way magic flowed out of grandfather's fingers. He had made the chimney. It was burning. He was astonished by what he had achieved. He was filled with wonder. He had seen a miracle with his own eyes.

Out of all the tools only the pencil had not betrayed him. He felt proud of the pencil.

He decided that he would keep it with him at all times. His eyes shone with happiness like stars. He wanted to cry, there were tears in his eyes. With trembling hands he picked up his burning chimney and placed it among the chimneys his grandfather had made.

His chimney stood apart among them. Burning bright. You could see it shine. A shining chimney.

The chimney shone like the stars. He felt some part of his grandfather inside himself. Maqbool was happy. Maqbool is happy. His eyes shine with the light of the stars.

Maqbool trembles with happiness.

His eyes fill up with water.

The water in his eyes makes the stars shine brighter still.

New Mother

Maqbool was six months old when he made his first journey. From Pandharpur to Indore. His grandfather had told him, or perhaps he had dreamt it.

Six year old Maqbool thought as he prepared to make his second journey. He had no memory of the first. So every step of the second became more important.

His father's third marriage and his first journey. A Gujarati mother. A stepmother. His heart was full of misgivings. He had heard many stories about stepmothers. In every story she was a witch. And every story was true.

Maqbool was excited. And the excitement caused the fear from those stories to fade away. He experienced many things for the first time in preparation for the wedding. He had been measured for an achkan. He would see a train for the first time. He would sit in one for the first time.

The train journey was not the only exciting part. The wedding feast, an unknown city, unknown people, the food during the journey, the new mother. He had many reasons to be thrilled.

Siddhpur. The wedding took place with great fanfare in this small town, or village rather, of Gujarat. The guests from the groom's side wore Turkish hats. There was a red hat for Maqbool as well. In his achkan's pocket he carried his magic pencil.

Exhausted by the spectacle of the wedding, the festivities, Maqbool didn't realise when he fell into the arms of sleep, lulled by the gentle rocking of the train.

Late at night, as if in a dream, Maqbool saw the bride's pale hands covered in henna. Two beautiful feet peeking out from under the red lehenga. Two big eyes, sleepy and full of sweetness. Like two shining stars.

A mother's eyes see the world and show you the world.

Was it in a dream or for real? He doesn't remember. But he saw the bride's face. His new mother's face. Shirin's face.

He met her only when they were back home. He was anxious. On the one hand were all the tales about witchy stepmothers, on the other was his new mother. It was as if there was a frightening invisible curtain between him and her, and even though he wanted to he couldn't push it aside to approach her.

The stepmother stories pushed him out of the house. He began to wander around all by himself. Not far from home, past the Parsi neighbourhood was the Naulakha garden. The Naulakha had nine lakh trees. He didn't even try to count. The river Khan flowed through the middle of the garden.

Maqbool loved to watch the calm flow of the water. There was a small island in the middle of the river and a wooden bridge to get to it. Maqbool would stand in the middle of the bridge and stare at the flowing water. He would watch shapes form and disappear. The shimmer, the water's blinding sheen attracted him. Because of the island the garden was also called 'the island garden'.

Nine lakh trees, and because of these trees many spots in the garden possessed the haziness of evening even during the day. Maqbool liked to stand in these shaded spots that lay shielded from the strong light of the sun. He would pass his days watching the day pass.

You had to cross a big road to get to the garden. Maqbool had heard that this was a national highway. From Bombay to Agra. Or from Agra to Bombay. A vehicle would pass now and then on the deserted road. Maqbool would often stand in the middle of the road and try to figure out which direction Bombay was in and which direction Agra was in. The road disappeared around a curve in both directions.

He wondered why one couldn't go to both Bombay and Agra at the same time.

As he left home and walked towards the garden, one of his favourite pastimes was to try and remember the route and recall the things he had seen along the way. He would recall the road signs, reconfigure them in his imagination and remember them again — that was how he dealt with his loneliness.

Standing on the bridge in the garden and watching the water flow. Calm on one side of the bridge and flowing and falling with great velocity on the other. Maqbool loved to watch and identify the shapes forming in the water. The same shapes appearing and disappearing again and again. Wandering through the forest. Listening carefully to every sound. Spending his whole day among the trees and plants. That was what he loved to do.

His new mother quickly assumed all responsibilities in the household. Maqbool was the youngest in the family. She loved him very much. Her pure heart and capable hands brought new light to the house.

His father's seriousness, his grandfather's steadfast love, his new mother's care — in spite of it all Maqbool would feel as if something, someone was missing.

He would feel that something somewhere was not in its right place. But he couldn't put a finger on what this something was. He would wander about anxiously. His heart would not be still. He would try to imagine how his mother was different from his new mother.

In this seeing, he would try to embellish the unseen.

An anxious Maqbool could be found wandering among the nine lakh trees of the Naulakha garden, searching for peace.

In the waters of the river Khan he saw a reflection of his mother. Every familiar shape was cloaked in a sheet of unfamiliarity. The whole world appeared familiar, then unfamiliar. Changing from moment to moment. Known one moment, unknown the next. The scene changing, becoming jumbled, scattering, becoming beautiful, everything happening as if for the first time.

Trees, plants, animals, birds would change form as he watched. Would acquire an unfamiliar form. Everything would fill up with a shining light. Overflowing with the unfamiliar white light of the stars. Everything would dissolve into everything else.

The familiar turned into the unfamiliar. The unfamiliar into the familiar.

The sunlight filtering through the leaves would uncover innumerable shapes hidden in the canopy. The translucent green of the leaves would appear to slowly throb. The sharp call of a peacock would pierce the silence. He would stop. Nature bound him. The sun would appear to saunter behind the colours that shone in its light. A seven coloured rainbow would drown and then resurface through the voice of the birds. The peacock's call would break into pieces and fall.

The strutting wind, the sauntering sun, the sight of all the sounds, he was feeling all this for the first time. There was a thrill in this. There was mystery. Maqbool would come here and forget everything. He wanted to be bound by this attraction. He would feel as if he was with his mother. That she was somewhere close and could appear at any time.

Mother is sunlight. Spreading brightness all around.

Mother is calling through the peacock.

Through the birds' calls she asks, 'How are you?'

Mother becomes the wind and whispers in his ears.

So softly that the words drift away before he can hear them.

Mother appears everywhere wearing a rainbow coloured stole.

He touches the peacock's call.

He catches hold of the sunlight playfully. Playing with them, talking to them, meeting them and then going away, fighting and arguing with them — Maqbool falls asleep as he does all this. He heads to the garden each day as if hypnotised. Listening to, smelling, touching, tasting and seeing nature.

When he feels hungry he remembers his new mother.

His new mother is very nice. When she talks to Maqbool she sometimes lapses into Gujarati. She loves feeding him and teaching him Gujarati. Maqbool likes the new language. He learns many words very quickly. He beings to like being with his new mother, sitting and eating with her. There is a sweetness in Shirin's hands and this sweetness rubs off on the food. He wants to spend as much time as possible with his new mother but the mysterious world of Naulakha keeps beckoning him and he quickly goes back to his own world.

Sometimes he will make a picture of his mother with his grandfather's magic pencil.

He makes many pictures of the garden.

Maqbool can't remember his mother's face.

The face of the garden keeps changing.

One thing in summer. Another in winter.

The rain-washed leaves deepen his understanding of colour.

He watches all this with quiet astonishment.

Sanyogitaganj & Studies in Baroda

After the death of his grandfather Maqbool became even more lonely. In the absence of his father, Maqbool's father Fida Husain became aware of his own age. He began to see his responsibilities as a father. Maqbool who until now had been a shadow walking around clutching his grandfather's finger suddenly seemed as large and real as a camel. He began to worry about Maqbool's studies. He decided to send him to Baroda so that he could get some religious education. He sent Maqbool with his younger brother Murad to an unknown land.

Maqbool was left at a boarding school in Baroda still reeling from the sadness of losing his grandfather. But he was soon happy after making new friends in this new place. He settled easily into the new environment.

Memories of the Naulakha garden, the road that went to neither Bombay nor Agra, the river Khan, his grandfather's workshop, the sweetness in his new mother's hands kept coming to him, sometimes strong, sometimes weak.

And as usual the miracles of Maqbool's magic pencil continued here as well. Before the school's drawing master Mohammed Ather could draw a bird on the blackboard it came and sat on Maqbool's slate. On the 2nd of October, Mahatma Gandhi's birthday, the day would begin with Maqbool drawing a picture on the blackboard.

Maulvi Akbar would make Maqbool learn a speech for the assembly of the madrasa. Maqbool would enact the speech with a full bevy of expressions and gestures. At the end of one speech was a Persian couplet:

Kasbe kamaal kun ki azeezat jahaan shavee

Kasbe kamaal niyaarzad azeeze man

Or:

Those who reach great heights in art are beloved by the world

Those who don't possess the wonder of art can't win any heart.

Maqbool would come first in all the games at the madrasa. Whether it was the high jump or kabaddi. He was a laggard only when it came to sprinting. His tall, slim physique blossomed here. At the same time the religious education at his maternal grandfather's home, the forty lessons in good behaviour and the twelve ways of purity cultivated a seriousness in him. Maqbool would learn and forget and learn again all thirty chapters of the Quran.

The Darultulba Madrasa was a school of the Husamia Sulaymani community. G.M. Hakim was in charge of running it. The teachers were Abbas Tayyabji, Maulvi Akbar, Keshavlal Gujarati and Major Abdul Pathan. Maqbool was the lone student. Guljama Khan was the bandmaster. Maqbool enjoyed Gulab Bawarchi's rotis along with his wife's meat curry.

Baroda was the second city he had lived in after Indore. Absolutely spick and span. With wide roads and trees. Innocence in the air. Maqbool, Mohammed Ibrahim Gauhar Ali, Abbasji Ahmed and Hamid Kambar Husain became deep friends. Different in nature and physique but united in their romanticism and vowing never to part.

The annual assembly of the madrasa was the centre of attraction for Maqbool, and Maqbool was the centre of the madrasa. Whether it was lessons or games or drawing or mischief, Maqbool took the prize in everything.

The annual assembly would end with a photograph of the invited guests and teachers being taken by Luqmani the photographer. As soon as Luqmani, wrapped in black cloth, focussing the camera, would say 'ready', Maqbool would jump into the frame. Maqbool began to take an interest in photography.

Maqbool's education progressed under the watchful care of his maternal grandfather in Gujarat. Living with his Nana he learned what control was. What discipline was. Here the daily routine was bound up in Nana's hard and fast rules and laws. He felt a seriousness beginning to fill him up. He was surprised at how Nana managed to enforce this strict discipline without behaving harshly. Every morning he went for a walk with Nana. Nana wasn't much of a talker. Maqbool's questions became the reason for him to talk.

After coming back from the morning walk he would read the Quran. In the beginning Maqbool's attention would wander. Sometimes to the khichdi, sometimes to the curry for lunch in the afternoon. He especially liked the rotla made of bajra. The food here was sweet. Like his new mother's. Sometimes his mind would wander to his father. To the Naulakha garden. The river Khan. The streets and alleys of the cantonment. The differences between Baroda and Indore. The memory of his grandfather. His mother's unknown face. The stars. The shining leaves. The peacock's call. The magical sunlight filtering through the leaves. The bridge in the garden. The shapes appearing and disappearing. They would all draw him towards them. Maqbool would try to concentrate. To focus his attention on reading.

His attention would wander. His eyes would keep slipping up amid the forms and the shapes of the verses. Gradually his attention began to get caught up in the sound of Nana's words. In a few days he found his own trembling voice following Nana's baritone. He would try to produce the same sort of power in his voice, the same rise and fall, the same seriousness but he found his small voice stumbling and powerless. From behind glasses, Nana's eyes would encourage his despairing, collapsing voice. Then with renewed zeal, moving and swaying, his eyes fixed on the verses, he would loudly begin to follow Nana's voice once more.

Gradually he began to enjoy reciting verses from the Quran. He was able to use his voice like an adept craftsman. He could see his voice soar. He would fly it to the Naulakha garden, spread it out upon the dry leaves like sunlight filtering through. He would make it dive into the river Khan. He would pause it near the shining stars, would move it again and again through the glistening leaves.

He'd move his voice behind Nana's voice sometimes and sometimes in front. Often he'd keep holding on to both voices like a bird that had stopped mid-flight. Now his voice didn't stumble nor did it break. In the clear light of his voice a glimmer of maturity began to appear. He was sad that his voice couldn't get the bass notes of Nana's voice no matter how hard he tried. But it also gave him satisfaction that in the wind of his voice Nana's voice could continually take flight.

Maqbool finished his studies and came back to Indore. The house had grown larger. He had two brothers and sisters. He suddenly felt older. Maqbool made many friends in Sanyogitaganj Higher Secondary School. He began to forge a relationship with the changed, new world around him. Acchan Mian's tea shop was still there but there seemed to be less light in the coals. No mystery remained in the Naulakha garden. There was still excitement, the river Khan was still inviting. His wandering continued as before. He went to a temple for the first time with Manakeshwar, a friend from school. He pretended to be Basant and watched as his friend prayed. This became a part of his daily routine. This was also when he heard the Ramayana being read out. The story of Ram shook Maqbool. In the voice coming from the pundit's throat he heard the same rhythms as in Nana's voice.

He recalled what he had learnt. In the beginning when he sat to learn the verses his mind would wander. His powers of concentration increased with strict discipline. It surprised him. Had this discipline always been inside him or was it a gift of the verses? He got the same feeling here. The rhythm of reading the verses from the Ramayana was also the same. He could not apprehend any forms in the world of these voices to begin with. Then slowly he would see them taking shape. As if coming out of the tip of a pencil. You could see them but not touch. You could know them but not recognise.

Maqbool had a lot of fun organising small athletic contests at school. The winners would get beautiful medals that he made by hand. Maqbool would give these medals novel shapes through hard work and imagination. It was here that Maqbool saw a Ramlila for the first time. A Ramlila was organised in the school grounds for nine days. Maqbool would go every evening and he noticed that many actors in the Ramlila belonged to his own neighbourhood. The paan seller Shankar's brother played Hanuman. Fat Mitthulal who sat at the flour mill played Ravana. The music belonged to Mian Kasim's band which he recognised very well. All their tunes were funereal. Maqbool also wanted to work in the Ramlila, to act. He wanted to go on stage but never got the opportunity.

But while watching the Ramlila Maqbool would start drawing scenes from it. He would be present in every character. He made many drawings of the Ramlila: *Maqbool's Ramlila.*

After the Ramlila Maqbool was introduced to cinema. His father Fida Husain was a film buff. But he'd strictly forbidden his family. They would only go to the movies twice a year. After Bakr Eid and after Sweet Eid. The day after the festival the whole family would go to watch a movie. Maqbool would find it very difficult to contain his excitement. Earlier he would have grabbed his grandfather's finger and taken tiny steps. Now his grandfather was no longer around. Sometimes he'd grab his father's finger. Then the realisation of being older made him walk all by himself. Fida Husain's family would go to the movies with great pomp. Shirin would go without a veil, the object of envy for every woman in the neighbourhood. Fida Husain was greatly respected so no one dared object.

Maqbool would lose himself in the walking and talking images. He found it amazing. A miracle. He wanted to see all the movies running in the city. But alas. Father had given strict instructions: two films only. He would have to rein himself in.

One night he lay in bed pretending to sleep. Father went out with new mother. Maqbool got up quietly and followed them to the cinema. When his father was about to buy the tickets he went and stood in front of him. His father bought three tickets instead of two and that year Maqbool watched three movies with his father. Slowly he began to watch more. He was clever enough to save time and money for watching new movies. When he came home he would draw scenes from the movie on paper with his magic pencil.

During the afternoon's study his mind would be focused on drawing Jamna's body. Jamna's body was still immune to the magic of Maqbool's pencil. Maqbool would stubbornly go after her every day when she would bathe in the river Khan after having finished the afternoon's chores. Maqbool would sit on the bank and sketch her. He had started diving into the river of sketching. A madness had gripped him. Maqbool would go to any place to sketch. Jamna was present in his sketches, the river Khan was present. The shapes that appeared and disappeared in the water were there too and he could see himself in the middle of it all, swimming, wandering.

Fida Husain was worried. Maqbool was growing older and didn't know any craft. What would he do when he grew up? One day he took Maqbool to Lal Khan the tailor and said, 'He draws well. He could make a good cutter. Teach him something.'

So that the boy could start earning.

On the first day Lal Khan gave him two needles and taught him the first lesson. Hold both needles in front of you and lift one up after the other like this, as if making an imaginary running stitch. Maqbool stared at Lal Khan and ran away making a rude gesture. For the first time in his life Maqbool felt hate.

Camera

Maqbool got carried away last Eid and climbed up the tree in the courtyard of the house with a camera. From atop the tree he took a picture of the celebrations in the courtyard. Over the past few years Fida Husain had become the head of a very large family, with his new wife, new kids and increased business. During festivals there would be a lot of hustle and bustle in the house just from the number of relatives. Then there were guests too.

There wasn't an empty corner in the whole courtyard. Maqbool took a picture. Fida Husain liked it very much. He began to see a budding photographer in his son and that made him very happy.

This Eid Maqbool got a Kodak camera as a present. It was the first present he'd received in his life.

His own camera.

He was happy, very happy. While giving him the camera his father had said, 'Who knows you might even be called to the palace to take a picture of the Maharaja someday!'

In his heart there was also the hope that if Maqbool learned something he might start earning too. Maqbool was happy. Even though his pictures couldn't walk like in the movies, he would still make them talk.

He used up the first roll in taking pictures of his younger sister Dilbar.

The camera that hung from Maqbool's shoulder excited his friends as well. Everyone looked forward to seeing something new. Maqbool had become known among his friends for his unique imagination and behaviour. All their hopes were now pinned on the shutter of the camera hanging from his shoulder.

And Maqbool did not want to disappoint them. But he needed some time. There were many ideas taking shape inside his head. He wanted to astonish his friends. His friendship with the camera was deepening. The pictures he took were never ordinary but Maqbool wanted to take a picture that would firmly establish his superiority among his friends.

There were many people in his house. Twenty or twenty-two. Every year his new mother's brothers' wives would give birth to one or two new members. Maqbool was getting more brothers and sisters every year. His responsibilities were increasing too. Food for the whole house was cooked in one kitchen. Maqbool was responsible for kneading dough for rotis. He would lose himself in the big pan, kneading dough for twenty-two people. He would take care that the flour and water mixed well in each and every corner of the pan. Not a speck could escape his fingers. He would make hundreds of shapes as he worked the dough and then knead them away.

A girl named Butul had been hired recently to help with chores around the house. Butul's mother worked in a neighbouring house. After Butul arrived Maqbool started to like working in the kitchen. Her full, exciting body, the churidar pyjama and tight kurta attracted him. Kneading dough became an excuse. Butul would scurry about doing all the housework.

Maqbool began to take more time with kneading the dough.

If Butul – with her narrow forehead, a silver chain around her neck and a sandalwood stud in her nose – ever smiled when she saw Maqbool he would end up putting either too much or too little water in the dough.

There had been a picnic at Pipliya Pala last fortnight and Maqbool had sat Butul on his father's bicycle and driven around the edge of the lake for a long time. After that Butul seemed scared. Perhaps it was because Maqbool had been careless in showing off, riding the bike without his hands on the handlebars. Whatever it was, Butul now kept her distance.

After that picnic the dough Maqbool kneaded began causing the rotis to crumble and break.

One afternoon Maqbool watched Butul put her little brother to sleep on a swing. As she rocked the swing she softly hummed something. Maqbool noticed there were not many people about that hot afternoon. Those that were there were in deep slumber. He felt his heart beat faster. He snuck into the room. Butul saw him but pretended not to and rocked the swing faster. Her humming slowed down. Maqbool felt a storm rising in his body.

Every corner of the house felt Butul's heat and the faltering of Maqbool's breath. That was the day he discovered touch.

With the new camera, Butul and his father's bicycle, Maqbool started flying. Sitting in front of him Butul could feel him soar. Maqbool told his friends to prepare to see some rare pictures. They were sure to be stunned. Maqbool's deeds were amazing.

He was going somewhere alone with a girl for the first time. Naulakha. The island garden. A new camera. His heart soaring. His breath ragged. There were two more reasons for his ragged breath: one, he was riding the cycle hard and two, Butul was heavier than he'd expected.

Maqbool is coming to the Naulakha garden for the first time with a girl. He is full of excitement. He is familiar with every nook and cranny of the garden. He takes her to all the places he especially likes. Butul under the open sky, in the middle of the garden, in nature. The whole roll is used up in a hurry. As he clicks the twelve frames

Maqbool keeps hoping all the while that the roll will never end. Finances won't permit him to get another one.

He showed Butul the whole garden. He told her stories of every tree he knew about. He also told her stories of all the trees he knew nothing about.

He wanted to spend the whole day with her. The film roll, the wandering, the talking, everything was over as if in a moment. The rest of the day loomed like a mountain before him. Maqbool couldn't believe how time had passed.

Depressed, Maqbool came back with Butul. His friends were waiting, Maqbool was waiting. His friends were impatiently waiting to see something wondrous. Maqbool was impatiently waiting to produce a wonder. Everyone went with him to get the roll washed.

***

'Shall we go to the ruins, Prabhash?' Maqbool asked.

Prabhash pretended not to hear.

'Shall we go to the ruins, Prabhash?' Maqbool said in a firmer voice this time. The tone was commanding yet hesitant. Prabhash who had been busy biting his fingernails until then pulled his hand out of his mouth and said, 'The ruins? No way. I won't go. Ghosts live there.'

There was fear and dread and excitement in his voice. Maqbool had heard the stories too. But he wanted to go. There was the fear of ghosts but a mischievous plan was forming in his mind.

The ruins were of a half built structure outside the city. The half palace of the Holkar kings. Ghostly stories of this forgotten building on the outskirts circulated through the city.

Riding their bicycles along the thick tree lined trails, talking, they didn't even realise how time passed and they reached the ruins.

They began to explore that ruined splendour. Even a small sound was enough to startle them in that desolation. They could hear the movement of air. There was a stench in the old basement. They kept exploring for a long time, kept looking.

There were no ghosts. When a dense darkness began to surround them in the basement they turned back. They saw bats dangling asleep as they returned. Crumbling and fallen walls. The sound of their footsteps on the raw, sand covered floor was making their hearts beat faster. They saw, they touched the ruined splendour and they came out. In the light of day they took deep breaths and exhaled deeply to push the stench out of their lungs.

'Hold the camera and keep a finger here. I'll be right back.'

Saying this and hanging the camera from Prabhash's neck Maqbool disappeared into the bushes.

It was deserted. No houses for miles. Prabhash stood in the middle of it all and cast a glance around. In the middle of these rattling, echoing ruins he stood all alone with a camera around his neck. There was no one for miles. He realised he had been standing alone for a long time. Maqbool had been gone a long time.

He became more and more convinced that there was no one else in the ruins but him and the ghosts.

The air was still.

The ruins were silent.

Maqbool had vanished.

There was no movement in the bushes.

Absolute silence.

He began to get scared. He was alone. Even the camera in his hand didn't give him any courage. He felt ashamed and also felt like laughing at his foolishness. But there was no time to laugh. He wanted to call out loudly to Maqbool. He tried but it felt like something had got stuck in his throat. He swallowed spit to try and wet his dry throat but nothing was going right.

Maqbool?

Maqbool!

He called out loudly but but there was no one else to hear.

Maqbool was nowhere.

Perhaps the sound was trapped somewhere. He tried again. No sound came out.

A boy clutching a camera in the middle of the ruins.

Such a strange sight! If someone saw him, what would they think? He felt like laughing.

A boy standing in the Holkar ruins, camera in hand.

He laughed.

He cried.

He wanted to call out. Something caught in his throat.

He wanted to run but couldn't move his feet.

He should have refused to take the camera.

He felt a cold sweat break out on his forehead.

His fear increased.

His heart beat faster.

He had been made a fool of.

Where was Maqbool?

Fear began to grip his heart.

He wanted to leave.

Then he saw. In front of him. A girl. Naked. Facing away from him. Long hair covering her back.

A ghost.

If he hadn't been holding the camera with both hands he would have rubbed his eyes in disbelief.

A naked girl right in front of him.

A ghost in the ruins. His mind froze.

'Take a picture. Press the shutter.'

He heard Maqbool's loud voice before anything could happen to him from seeing this ghost in the ruins.

Mechanically he pressed he shutter. The click echoed in the silence.

Prabhash wanted to control the camera. The loud click startled him. He looked towards the girl, but what's this? She had vanished!

He looked all around. She was nowhere to be seen.

Prabhash was scared.

He was sure now. He had been trapped by ghosts.

He tried to remember the sequence of events.

Maqbool's disappearance.

The air becoming still.

The ruins falling silent.

The lack of movement in the bushes.

Losing his voice.

His feet getting stuck.

The naked girl.

Maqbool's disembodied command.

The vanishing girl.

What had happened?

How would he escape from this maze of ghosts?

He wanted to run. Where was Maqbool? How could he leave him alone? If he took the cycle, how would Maqbool come? Where should he keep the camera? Should he leave it or take it with him? Maqbool would be angry. He would fight with Maqbool.

Prabhash's thoughts were racing, chased by ghosts.

No one would believe what had happened to him in these desolate ruins.

Who believes in ghosts?

But he had seen one.

He had taken a picture of one.

Would Maqbool give him the photo?

Maqbool.

There he was, in front of him, smiling.

What would Prabhash do?

He suddenly felt alive again.

Maqbool came from the same spot where the girl had been.

He came and took the camera.

Prabhash quickly told him all that had happened. Maqbool kept laughing. Kept taking pictures of this and that. Prabhash couldn't believe it. Maqbool was listening to everything calmly. Laughing at everything. His hair was open.

Some days later he showed his friends the picture of the naked girl in the ruins. It took their breaths away.

Maqbool's picture had spoken.

Malwa

Fida Husain's growing family and his growing children meant that Maqbool's responsibilities were also growing. Now he would knead the dough and also make the rotis. Fida Husain would often watch him as he worked in the kitchen. He wanted Maqbool to either draw pictures or take photographs.

Busy with chores in the kitchen Maqbool couldn't think of doing anything else.

Everyone in the house knew that Maqbool loved drawing pictures.

One afternoon Fida Husain declared that Maqbool would live in the adjoining building from now on. He had rented a room in that building for Maqbool. There he could work as he pleased. Someone else would have to make the rotis.

Maqbool was happy. A room of his own. His own place where he could live as he pleased, come and go as he pleased, make pictures as he pleased.

Make pictures all day.

Someone else was responsible for the rotis now.

That was also when he began to learn English from his father's friend Farhat Ali. Farhat Ali gave him many books to read and Maqbool would have to hide them from his father. His father didn't think that one should read any book besides the Revealed Book. He thought romantic and emotional stories had a bad effect on children.

He never told Maqbool any story when he was a child.

Maqbool spent his childhood drawing heroes from stories.

In these stories his mother was the princess.

No one had seen the princess in the story.

In his image of the princess was his mother.

In his image of his mother was the princess.

Maqbool began to get more and more interested in reading. He began to go to the library of Christian College with his friends.

They had a great collection of books there.

Poems, plays, stories, novels.

Maqbool would read like crazy. He would go and sit in the English classes.

He saw pictures of Avanendranath Tagore, Nandlal Bose, Chugtai.

He discovered Rembrandt, Turner, Velazquez. These books encouraged him. He saw their work and learned the finer details of painting. And in the light of the first lamp he'd made at Dada's workshop, he began to make perfect copies of these paintings.

Everyone would praise these pictures.

Maqbool wanted to learn more about these painters. But there were almost no books in the library on art.

Around this time he also convinced his father to let him learn Urdu poetry.

Seeing how he was getting busier his father bought him a bicycle. Maqbool's wanderings grew further and longer.

Going to the surrounding villages to draw the landscape became a part of his daily routine.

Malwa's dusty landscape and the women in this landscape with their vibrant dresses — the juxtaposition fascinated him.

Mixing vibrant and dusty colours became one of his favourite pastimes.

***

Maqbool's activities increased.

His interests increased.

His wanderings increased.

His patience decreased.

He began to play hockey.

He began to play football for Usha Club.

He began to play tennis with his father.

He continued organising small contests and making medals with his own hands.

He entered one of his paintings in the Holkar State Painting Exhibition. It would be the first public exhibition of his work. He hoped that everyone would like it. He had painted a landscape of Malwa especially for the contest.

Malwa's dusty colour.

A scene covered in Malwa dust.

Passing through the landscape were women wrapped up in vibrant dresses.

Trees swayed like stains in the scene's expanse.

There was no limit to Maqbool's imagination.

The painting became the landscape.

Maqbool was busy all the time.

Studying at Christian College.

Learning poetry at the Ustad's house.

Playing at the Sanyogitaganj School grounds.

Learning English if Farhat Ali's mood permitted.

Playing football if Madan brought one along.

Going to the tennis court with his father.

For all this he had to depend on someone else. But for painting he only needed the ever present light of his magical lamp.

He could start wherever he wanted.

He could start whenever he wanted.

He didn't need anyone else to make a painting.

Just solitude. And there was no better solitude than that of his own room.

But he also wanted to do everything else. And so, to maintain a balance, his daily routine turned into a nightly routine.

As soon as night fell he would take his painting equipment and a lantern and head to the villages outside the city. Making landscapes in the night gave him a new kind of excitement. All the colours, vibrant, red and dusty got mixed up in the dark.

In the night all colours look the same. He applies colours by approximation. Red he thinks and then applies red.

Applying black in the dark is like touching darkness.

It was a game that he began to enjoy. Interesting mistakes would occur as he did this. Using his instinct he would apply the colour again.

He began to get to know colours for real.

In the colours of his imagination he began to fill in the colours of truth.

They were not at all similar.

Applying the colour at night and seeing it in the light of day became a surprise he used to wait for.

The night's landscape would change during the day.

The night's colours were not the colours of day.

He began to work hard so that the colours of night and day could become one.

He constantly learned and discarded, discarded and learned.

His powers of concentration became intensely focussed.

He began to know the true nature of colours. He began to imagine colours.

The colours applied at night would change during the day.

During the daytime he would compare his painting with the real landscape.

His approximations and instincts would turn out to have been wrong.

Slowly he learned that the only use for the lantern was to find a place to sit, to set up his workspace and so on. Then he would keep it at some distance.

This meant that the hovering insects would also keep away.

In the darkness he would look at the dark, learn to recognise the colours, absorb them into his soul before he even began to make a painting.

He was testing the idea that the shapes of darkness would take shape in the painting on their own.

It was the power of darkness to dissolve shapes into one another.

To make them difficult to identify.

Familiar shapes would become unfamiliar. They were visible but he couldn't see them.

The colours too fared no better. You couldn't tell where they had disappeared. All of them looked the same.

They hesitated to reveal themselves in the low light of the lantern.

He had some feeling for colour based on his experience of seeing during the day but inexperience would clog up his palette. Darkness would cloud the identity of colours.

Maqbool would try to set experience aside and focus on making what he could see now.

He would avoid drawing what he saw in the day.

To see what was unseen in the night was the challenge he had set himself.

But in the light of day the night's work looked lifeless.

He would try. To see properly.

To select the right colours.

In the cloudy darkness he would keep his first magical lamp lit. In the dark of night two shining stars would keep watch over him. He would feel his mother's blessings upon him. As though she were watching him in the night. The day's Maqbool was Fida Husain's son. His father took care of his upbringing. And he worried about when he would start earning.

***

Around this time, Maqbool's father opened a general store for his younger brother Murad in Ranipura. Maqbool was ordered to mind the store on Sundays.

His busy life became busier still.

He'd sit in the store all day and cause his uncle losses. The result was that the store had to be shut. A clothes shop was opened instead. That too suffered the same fate. Maqbool would be lost in drawing pictures. Cows would eat the cloth.

Earlier Maqbool would mind the store during holidays. Now his uncle would. Maqbool's attention was on painting. His uncle's attention was nowhere at all. Maqbool couldn't even remember when the clothes shop turned into a restaurant. But he found it more convenient to paint sitting at the restaurant counter.

Maqbool's wanderings couldn't be stopped for too long. The restaurant too was close to being shut.

Whenever Maqbool got the chance he would run off. His father had a shirt stitched for him with many pockets. In these pockets he would keep all the things he needed, colours, brushes, pencils, etc.

He made many paintings of Bartan Bazar, Big Sarafa, Small Sarafa, Marethiya Bazar, Lal Kuan, Bombay Bazar, Harsiddhi, Old Indore…

One day in the midst of his wanderings he came to Bartan Bazar. And he saw that there was someone else besides him making a picture.

Maqbool quietly went and stood behind him.

That person was calmly sketching the scene at Bartan Bazar. Maqbool's attention went to the paper. It wasn't white like he was used to. It was a light grey paper on which colours were being layered slowly, one after the other.

Maqbool liked this technique. One colour on top of another and on top of that yet another. This was something new. First the deeper colours then the lighter ones. The colours were being applied in reverse. Maqbool watched intently.

The colours were the same as what he used.

But this person was using colours in his own way.

Gradually the scene began to emerge.

He wasn't filling colours into a drawing, instead the shapes were emerging from the colours.

Everything was in the painting. Exactly the same.

He saw that unnecessary details had been ignored.

Shapes had not been drawn but they were visible nonetheless.

He was looking intently.

His focus was broken when a loud, sharp voice asked, 'Why, do you also paint?'

'Yes.'

'What's your name?'

'Maqbool.'

'Bendre. My name is Narayan Shridhar Bendre.'

'You apply colours really well.'

'What did you think of my painting?'

'It's very good. Will you teach me?'

'Who do you learn from?'

'No one. Will you teach me? You apply colours really well.'

'No. First I'll see how you sketch.'

'Come. My house is in the cantonment.'

'Not now. I'll come later.'

'But where should I meet you?'

'Anywhere.'

Maqbool was desperate. He wanted Bendre to come home right away. This was the first time he had the chance to show a real painter his work. He didn't want to lose it.

Bendre did come home many days later. He saw Maqbool's pictures and was very impressed by them. For a long time he kept talking about painting.

Meanwhile, Maqbool had got a gold medal in the Holkar State Exhibition.

That painting affected Bendre very much. In fact that was why he came to visit Maqbool.

Maqbool and Bendre became great friends.

Bendre taught Maqbool how to practice.

They would talk about painting all day.

Maqbool learned how to apply colours. He learned the difference between water colours and oils. He went to art school with Bendre. There he saw the work of many painters and met his own contemporaries. He liked the atmosphere there. He also got to see many books on art.

Maqbool started coming to art school regularly.

Gossiping with friends, talking about art and meeting with Bendre were the reasons.

Maqbool had Bendre meet his father.

'Why don't you send him to art school?'

'Will he be able to do anything?'

'He has skill in his hands. A very keen intelligence. You should definitely send him to art school.'

Fida Husain had seen by now that Maqbool's true calling lay in painting. The gold medal he got in the Holkar State Exhibition only confirmed this. He agreed with what Bendre said.

Maqbool got admitted to the Indore School of Art.

Bendre was in the third year.

Nothing was new here for Maqbool except the atmosphere of the school. Whatever was being taught there was a piece of cake. The other students made one painting in many days. He made many paintings in one day. It was as if he was possessed.

Making sketches.

Reading books.

Looking at paintings.

Talking about other's paintings.

Time would pass quickly in all this.

In the night Maqbool would take his bicycle and lantern and go about his nightly routine.

***

The lines of Dattatreya Damodar Devlalikar, the school principal, attracted Maqbool. There was a simplicity in them, they had a quiet glory. His gaze would get caught up in their web. He could see the power in the curving of simple lines.

With his friends from school during the day and by himself at night Maqbool painted all the villages, hamlets and towns of the Malwa region.

Bendre's knowledge and Devlalikar's purity began to come together in his brush.

Maqbool used oil colours for the first time. His father brought him Winsor & Newton paints. He was still new to the pleasure of making an oil painting when someone bought one of the paintings he had made in Bartan Bazar.

Maqbool was happy. Everyone used to praise his work. But there was also a sadness in him. Sometimes his friends used to call him Husain instead of Maqbool. In conversation too they would call him Husain.

'Husain made a very good painting of Khajrana.'

'Husain, shall we go to Mandu?'

'Husain likes Ujjain very much.'

'Husain made a beautiful painting on a village wall in Patalpani.'

'Husain, will you come to eat a raou kachori?'

His friends would say. They would praise Husain but Maqbool didn't know who Husain was.

His friends were unknowingly making him feel more and more alone.

Maqbool's heart wasn't feeling at home in art school.

Maqbool was feeling lost.

Maqbool began to wander.

The distance between Maqbool and Husain only increased.

'He has wheels for feet,' people who knew him said.

Maqbool was restless.

Maqbool would try to be patient.

'Patience is Allah's greatest gift.'

He would remember what his grandfather used to say.

Maqbool was impatient.

Heaps of painting. Constant wandering. His hands didn't stop. His feet didn't tire.

His heart didn't fail.

His body didn't desert him.

Making and looking at pictures constantly would fill him up with an unknown power.

People began to notice him.

But he felt as if he was stuck.

And he knew only one way to get rid of this feeling.

To constantly make paintings.

Maqbool was helpless.

Impatient.

Attentive yet careless.

Selfless.

With no regrets.

All attention and astonishment, he would wander about looking at the landscapes of Malwa.

One evening Maqbool ended up on that road in the middle of Naulakha that went nowhere.

It had been there for many years, one side going to Agra and the other side going to Bombay. Now Husain knew that the side going towards the bridge was the side that went to Bombay.

Across the river Khan another world was waiting for him.

Maqbool left Indore – with his dreams, with his feelings, with God.

A New Beginning

Maqbool. Mumbai. Fate.

Maqbool. Mumba Devi. Fate.

There was no shelter for Husain in Bombay.

And more than shelter, he needed work. Wandering all day in search of work, meeting new people and making conversation without reason became a necessity. He found that here even strangers talked with intimacy. He found it difficult. He found it strange. The intimacy of strangers.

A strange intimacy.

He had no identity here.

He had no work. He would wander all day and sleep on footpaths in the night. How not to get lost in the crowd, that was the question.

There was another problem. How to see himself as a stranger. He began to recognise himself as Husain. In Indore he was Maqbool. Here no one called him that.

Husain.

He often felt as if it wasn't him but someone else they were calling. As if it wasn't him but some Husain they were talking to.

M.F. Husain.

Maqbool hid behind that M.

Calling someone by their name was uncultured. It was rude.

So his name became Husain.

Some friends called him M.F.

He craved to hear someone say Maqbool.

But no one here was interested in the words behind the M.F. In all these days no one had even asked him his full name.

But identity couldn't remain a problem for too long.

The problem of eating.

The problem of sleeping.

The problem of earning a living. These were bigger and more urgent.

It has been three years since Husain came to Bombay. In these three years he has made a place for himself. He's sent by film studios in Dadar and Andheri to make hoardings throughout the city. Sometimes he even gets to make hoardings for new films. In these three years he has made hundreds of hoardings in every corner of the city.

With his ladder, bicycle and paintbrush, Husain brought Suraiya, Kananbala, Kundanlal, Jamunadevi to life.

Often he'd have no chappals on his feet.

There were two reasons for that.

One, he didn't have the money.

Two, the chappals would wear out too quickly.

Sometimes he would wear them, sometimes not.

Bombay's dry, flat roads.

On these hot, cracking roads his burning feet would remind him.

Of his wanderings.

Of his stagnation.

And at last in 1964, during Gajanan Madhav Muktibodh's funeral procession, Husain vowed to never wear chappals again.

The money he earned was enough to provide him food and shelter.

Husain's attentive eyes, his practised hands and his incredible speed meant that he could complete the biggest banners in the blink of an eye.

His expertise, clarity and readiness to work came in for praise.

People became fans of his art.

Even those who were jealous of his talent would be enchanted by his work.

Until now his glory had been limited only to cinema hoardings.

The chance of his own work being appreciated didn't even look like a remote possibility.

But Husain did not despair or get sad.

Husain's burning feet on Bombay's roads.

They lit his magical lamp.

And the appreciation he got kept this lamp burning.

***

Indifferent to praise, Husain meanwhile was captivated by the spontaneous birth of a third form in the proximity of two forms.

He also made some friends.

He had no place to stay. Some nights he would spend at the homes of his friends, other nights he would stay out making hoardings and go to sleep right there whenever he was tired. And as soon as he woke in the morning he would begin working on the hoarding again.

The hoarding and Husain were one.

He was afraid his name might turn into Hoarding Husain.

He wanted to remain Maqbool.

No one called him Maqbool.

Bombay was full of unknown people hiding behind unknown names.

There was no star filled sky overhead.

It wasn't possible to see even two shining stars.

Husain had more than a few difficulties.

And there was not enough work to make them go away.

But like Abhimanyu, steadfast in his vow, he kept forging ahead through the chakravyuha of life.

He wanted to fill his paintings with the truth he gleaned from knowing and understanding life deeply, from hearing its rhythms and singing along. He had neither the cunning required to escape the chakravyuha nor the desire.

He had time but not patience.

Badarbagh. The Sulaymani building in Badarbagh. This was where many families of the Sulaymani clan lived. There was a large wall here against which Husain would prop up his hoardings to prepare. The people who lived here became his friends. They watched him draw film stars. His attractive personality. His seriousness about his art. His openness. He quickly became familiar among the people living there.

Mehmooda Bibi lived with her daughter Fazila and her son Khurshid on the second floor of a building overlooking the courtyard where Husain worked. From her window she would often watch this young man absorbed in his work. His tall, thin body. His black beard and long hair. The amazing speed with which he painted.

Eventually Husain realised that there were two eyes watching over him.

Two eyes that wished him well.

He felt a pang in his heart.

He felt the sky was full of stars once again and that they shone upon him.

Two shining stars in the sky were staring at him.

There was warmth in the yellow sunlight again.

There was the rustle of wind in the green leaves again.

He began to feel the presence of his mother.

In this unfamiliar city he felt for the first time a kindred presence. As soon as he stepped into the Sulaymani building, he stepped into the embrace of this special feeling.

For the first time in Bombay he found peace.

For the first time he did not feel a stranger.

He felt as if something life changing was about to happen. He felt safe.

He began to buy painting supplies from the money he earned from making hoardings and started painting at night. When he came here he felt as if his mother was watching him paint.

Was caressing his head. Husain felt secure with this maternal presence that surrounded him.

All apprehensions fled his heart. He began to believe in himself once more. To an extent he had never felt before.

There was zeal in his eyes, madness, desire.

Those shining stars swam before eyes.

He felt the burning lava inside him begin to flow.

Now he was unworried.

Unafraid.

A new power had come to reside in his hands.

He could turn the whole world upside down.

He did not need to see an image to paint it. If he could think it he could paint it. When he drew Kananbala he just had to think of her and the picture would get made.

In the courtyard of the Sulaymani building he found a sense of divinity and a sense of self.

The eyes watching over him were Mehmooda Bibi's.

They were filled with motherly love.

She worried about him and wanted to talk to him.

Maqbool could feel the presence of a mother.

One afternoon she called him home for lunch. Husain climbed the stairs to her flat, hesitant and confident at the same time, filled with some unknown trepidation.

He felt the same sense of security he had felt as he wandered about in the Naulakha gardens.

He knocked softly.

Mehmooda Bibi opened the door and greeted him happily saying, 'Come Maqbool, come inside.'

Maqbool.

Husain felt as if his heart had begun to beat again. It was the first time since coming to Bombay that he was hearing his name. It felt as if his mother had called out to him. He tried to see her face in Mehmooda Bibi's face.

He saw her two shining eyes.

Eyes filled with motherly love.

'Come Maqbool, come inside. May god keep you safe. There's magic in your hands. It's a miracle. When I see you paint, I pray to god. May god grant you bounties. Send your art to all corners of the world. May you be celebrated the world over.'

'Masha Allah, your paintings, there's magic in them.'

'My heart wants to keep looking at you. May all your bad luck descend upon me.'

Husain hadn't found anyone in Bombay who spoke with such sincerity. He hadn't found anyone who asked god for his happiness with such selflessness.

Loneliness had been his only companion here.

It was the first time someone here had taken his name with love. Blessed him.

Asked to take on his misfortunes.

His eyes filled with tears.

'Amma, you are the first person in Bombay who has called me Maqbool. For the first time I realised that I had been alone so far. You have loved me like a mother. I am grateful.'

'Maqbool, you should never think you are alone. I will give you an amulet. But eat something first.'

He was served food. Mehmooda Bibi sat beside him, insisting that he eat more.

Home cooked food. A mother's heart. Mehmooda Bibi's loving insistence.

Maqbool was in heaven.

He had never expected such love.

After he had eaten Mehmooda Bibi tied the amulet around his wrist and blessed him.

Maqbool had found home.

He kept his head in his mother's lap.

The shining stars were back in the sky.

Mehmooda Bibi kept on talking to Maqbool.

He felt intoxicated.

Six hours ago Maqbool had found a house in Bombay. He was able to save enough to afford a garage in Moreland that belonged to one Usman Bhai. He would try to get as much work as possible by making rounds of all the studios. He earned four annas per square foot for his hoardings. Most of the money had to be spent on cloth and colour. He began to make the wooden frames himself to save money.

He went eagerly twice a day to eat at Mehmooda Bibi's. He had found a place in Bombay where he felt safe and protected.

Around this time he began to realise that his eagerness was more to see Mehmooda Bibi's daughter Fazila than for the food.

There was an attraction between the two of them. As he made the banners he would feel a gaze upon him. When he turned he found her two shining eyes.

One day he went to the rooftop. He saw a girl leaning over the parapet trying to peer at his hoardings. It was Fazila.

Husain said, 'It's Friday tomorrow. Amma will go to have the Fatiha read at Maulvi sahib's place before going for the namaz at sunset. Keep a red soap box in the balcony when she leaves. I want to meet you alone. There's something I have to tell you.'

His tone was clear and measured. He couldn't believe how calm he sounded.

After that meeting on Friday all three buildings in Badarbagh became witness to Maqbool and Fazila's blossoming love.

Mehmooda Bibi decided to get them married.

Many people tried to dissuade her. What did she see in this ragged, unemployed man that she was arranging a match for her daughter with him?

There were as many opinions as there were people.

Unaware of all this Maqbool and Fazila kept seeking out excuses to meet.

The refined Fazila was enamoured more by the free-thinking mind of her carefree young husband-to-be than his talent.

She felt his way of thinking was unique.

She felt his every gesture was wondrous.

They would both wander in their sky of dreams.

Both would remain lost in thought.

Whatever the matter, Husain would never impose his thoughts.

Instead he was gently persuasive.

Nothing could stand in the way of his will.

Their two hearts were in love and didn't care about anything else.

But they would not fly into the unknown.

Husain was modest.

His wedding date was fixed.

Fazila

Husain's visits to Mehmooda Bibi's house increased. He began spending mealtimes and times of leisure there.

It was there that he got acquainted with a mother's love and affection.

Mehmooda Bibi felt that Maqbool was a suitable husband for her daughter.

She fixed their wedding date for 11 March 1941.

***

It's Husain's wedding today. He hasn't sent news of it to Indore. He's painting a banner for the film *Lagan* in order to earn some extra money. And while Kananbala's face gradually emerges against the sky, Maqbool's heart wanders in the Sulaymani building and the Naulakha garden.

He finishes the banner and takes the payment. For the first time in all his years in Bombay he takes a taxi and heads to Badarbagh to get to his wedding.

On the way he buys a pack of incense sticks – the only thing missing from the things he has collected for his new home.

The house was provided by his friend Mohammed Nasir, a postman who lived in Yemeni building. Mohammed Nasir lived alone in a two room house and felt he could let out the extra room to Husain.

And this room was more than enough for Husain's household. He liked the room. Together they collected some essential items. A bed, a chair, a table. Some things for the kitchen, a stove, a pot, a few essential utensils.

Beyond this, they decided, the bride would bring whatever she liked.

Nasir got the holy Quran and a bookstand for their wedding gift. Only the incense sticks were missing.

The room was cleaned.

It was arranged and rearranged.

They kept talking until late at night.

Husain felt something strange when he saw this clean and tidy, settled home. When he had left Indore he had no idea that he'd be getting married or setting up house in Bombay.

The wedding's tomorrow, he thought.

And now it was the day of the wedding. He could see that some guests had already arrived. He didn't know what arrangements needed to be made for the wedding and those who did know had made the arrangements yesterday. Only the incense sticks remained, so he brought those.

Mehmooda Bibi had made the arrangements very tastefully.

For a mahr of rupees forty, Husain was wedded to Mehmooda Bibi's daughter Fazila in a simple ceremony.

Maqbool came face to face with a new, unknown life.

Scenes from his father's wedding floated before his eyes.

The red Turkish hats. Everyone wearing red Turkish hats and standing at the railway platform in Siddhpur.

No one was wearing those hats here.

There the wedding procession went in a train, eating and drinking, joking and laughing the entire way.

Here people trickled in, about six or seven in all.

There, there was a brass band and music, there were lights and fancy food. Everyone was all dressed up. His father wore a turban.

Here everything was just as it was on any other day. Nothing had changed.

The guests came wearing white.

The wedding was a simple one held in a mosque.

People congratulated them, gave gifts and embraced them.

Husain was eager to see his bride.

After taking leave of his friends who were still celebrating, Husain stepped into his home late at night. Two stars shone in the black sky.

His first steps in his new home.

His first steps in his new life.

His bride had inspected the new house many times over while she waited.

With kohl lined eyes she watched Husain enter.

A new household, a new bride, a new groom. They would spend the rest of the night talking and dreaming new dreams.

Over the nightlong conversation Fazila would find out that waiting for Husain to come home was to become the foundation of her world.

***

Husain's wedding didn't cause any great changes in his life. Although some things did change. He turned the loft into a studio.

The house began to fill up with the smell of linseed oil.